DESMOND COLE
GHOST PATROL
THE VAMPIRE ATE MY HOMEWORK

by Andres Miedoso
illustrated by Victor Rivas

LITTLE SIMON

New York   London   Toronto   Sydney   New Delhi

LITTLE SIMON
An imprint of
Simon & Schuster Children's Publishing Division
1230 Avenue of the Americas, New York, New York 10020
First Little Simon paperback edition March 2021
Copyright © 2021 by Simon & Schuster, Inc.
Also available in a Little Simon hardcover edition.
All rights reserved, including the right of reproduction
in whole or in part in any form.
LITTLE SIMON is a registered trademark of Simon & Schuster, Inc.,
and associated colophon is a trademark of Simon & Schuster, Inc.
For information about special discounts for bulk purchases, please contact
Simon & Schuster Special Sales at 1-866-506-1949 or
business@simonandschuster.com.
The Simon & Schuster Speakers Bureau can bring authors to your
live event. For more information or to book an event contact the
Simon & Schuster Speakers Bureau at 1-866-248-3049
or visit our website at www.simonspeakers.com.
Designed by Steve Scott
Manufactured in the United States of America 0221 MTN
2 4 6 8 10 9 7 5 3 1
This book has been cataloged with the Library of Congress.
ISBN 978-1-5344-8283-8 (hc)
ISBN 978-1-5344-8282-1 (pbk)
ISBN 978-1-5344-8284-5 (eBook)

CONTENTS

CHAPTER ONE

CLASS-TROPHOBIA

Have you ever heard of class-trophobia? You pronounce it class-truh-fow-bee-uh. It's a made-up word for a very real problem.

Kids with class-trophobia are super-duper nervous about school stuff . . . like, *all* school stuff.

They dread not having enough pencils. They tremble if a teacher says, "Pop quiz."

And if they have to give a speech in class, they totally have *that* nightmare. The one about showing up to school in their pajamas.

And not just *any* pajamas. No, they're wearing their footsie pajamas with baby sheep all over them. Yikes!

When you go to a school like mine, there's a lot of class-trophobia.

Let me explain.

I live in a town called Kersville. It looks perfectly normal, but the truth is, it's haunted. Don't believe me?

Ask the ghost living in my house about it. His name is Zax, and he's pretty cool.

The Kersville library is haunted too. There are creepy mersurfers at the beach, a zombie zookeeper, and monsters cooking in our cafeteria.

We even had a real-life Boogie Man crash our school dance.

And why wouldn't he? I mean, just look at my school. Kersville Elementary is totally terrifying.

A long time ago it used to be a mansion, and now I'm pretty sure every hallway is haunted.

And yet I've never felt classtrophobia . . . until today.

That's me, Andres Miedoso. I'm the one covered in globby cheese and running for my life.

ANDRES MIEDOSO

And that is my best friend, Desmond Cole, holding the crustiest of crusty French bread in his hands like a couple of swords.

I bet you're wondering what we're doing, right? Well, that's a long and surprisingly *yummy* story that started yesterday.

DESMOND COLE

CHAPTER TWO

DR. ACKULA'S CASTLE

HiSSSSSS

Desmond and I were reading in class when our teacher hissed at us.

Our teacher's name is Dr. Ackula, and he is a little, um, *different*.

For example, when we get an answer right on a test, he puts a green *X* next to it.

And when we get an answer wrong, he puts a red check.

Talk about confusing! I fainted the first time I got a test back.

Not only that, but Dr. Ackula calls our classroom a castle, and he means it! No, there isn't a drawbridge or a moat with alligators. And there isn't a dungeon . . . at least we hope there isn't a dungeon.

Actually, the only thing that looks like it belongs in a castle is the creepy candlestick on Dr. Ackula's desk. It sits next to our class pet.

Yep, Dr. Ackula doesn't have a normal class pet like a hamster. Our class pet lives in a cage that is always covered.

In fact, none of us have ever seen what kind of animal is under there.

Whatever it is, it sleeps all the time—even through all our class noise. But if anyone gets near the cage, Dr. Ackula tells us not to disturb *his friend.*

It is all too weird.

Another thing that makes our teacher different is if our class gets too loud, he never turns off the lights like normal teachers. Oh no.

He just hisses the hissiest hiss you've ever heard! Sounds silly, but it sends shivers down our spines, and we quiet down faster than fast.

And that day, with five minutes left in school, Dr. Ackula hissed and everyone stopped talking.

"Now that I have your attention," he said, "I have an announcement. Tonight you will each work on a special homework project. And it's due tomorrow."

Talk about instant class-trophobia!

CHAPTER THREE

FAMILY FOOD DAY

It was easy to tell who was starting to panic in class.

First there was the eraser eater, Marshall Smith. He had stuffed way too many pencils in his mouth.

Lena Carter was a hair twirler, but now she'd tied her hair in a bow.

And I don't even want to tell you
what Emmanuel "nose picker" Neal
was doing. But I'm sure you could
guess!

The class waited and waited for Dr. Ackula to explain the project. But our teacher just sat there with an evil smirk on his face. He really enjoyed watching everybody freak out!

Do not Disturb

Finally we couldn't take it any-more. Everyone had questions.

"Will we need to wash our hands?" asked Emmanuel.

"Or tie knots?" added Lena.

"Will we need pencils?" Marshall mumbled.

Dr. Ackula held up his hands and answered the kids.

"Yes, maybe, and no," he said. "We are going to have our first Family Food Day. Students will cook a family recipe at home tonight and bring it to class tomorrow to share."

Hey, that project didn't sound bad at all! A huge sigh of relief from the whole class filled the room. Well, almost the whole class.

Desmond looked like he was about to cry. Which is weird because he's the bravest kid I know.

"Um, Dr. Ackula?" Desmond asked. "Do we have to make the food *with* our parents?"

"Yes," Dr. Ackula replied. "Time spent in the kitchen with your family is very important."

"Oh no," Desmond mumbled as he slumped over his desk like a puppet who had gotten its strings cut.

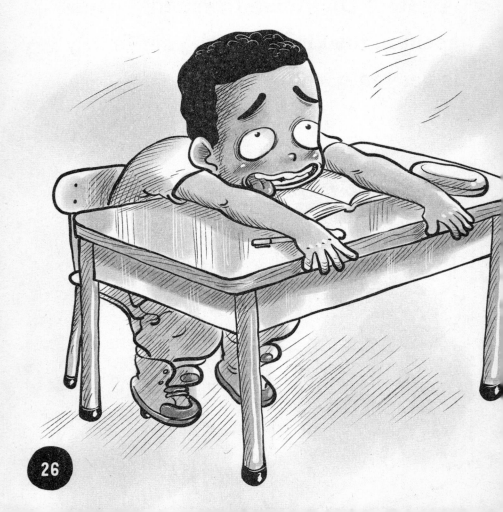

I knew what was going through his mind. See, Desmond's parents are the best, but they are *not* the best cooks in the world. In fact, they may be the worst cooks ever!

I mean, they eat anything. Green Jell-O with hard-boiled eggs and jellyfish. Lasagna with pickles and sardines. Oh, and burnt-bottom meat loaf with ostrich toes. I almost broke my tooth taking a thank-you bite of that one!

If Desmond brought that kind of food to class, everyone was going straight to the nurse's office.

As my best friend lay there like a slug, the other kids talked about what they were going to make.

I was excited too. Most of all, I was relieved. I thought Dr. Ackula was going to give us a test like that time he made us do push-ups and math at the same time.

But no! This was a way better homework assignment. All we had to do was cook yummy food. What's the worst that could happen?

The final bell rang, and students
jumped up to leave. But Dr. Ackula
stopped us with another hiss.

"Class, I have one last request," he said. "I've been very hungry lately. Not even my blood-orange-and-bone-marrow smoothies can fill me up."

He picked up the cup on his desk and took a gulp of thick red sludge. The slurping sounds made my skin crawl.

"So," Dr. Ackula continued, "DO NOT let me down! I am looking forward to eating all of you—I mean, all of your food tomorrow."

CHAPTER FOUR

HOME WRECK

"Cheer up," I told Desmond as we rode our bikes home after school. "It's not going to be *that* bad."

"Not for you, Andres," he said, getting his balance back. "*Your* parents are good cooks. They're the complete opposite of mine."

Desmond was deep in thought as he rode his bike.

"Look out!" I yelled as Desmond almost crashed into a giant oak tree.

He swerved around it just in time. *Whew!*

"Stop worrying," I told him. "Maybe we can find an easy recipe that your parents can't mess up. Like popcorn."

But Desmond's face turned green. "Uh, did I ever tell about the time my dad made ghost-pepper-and-grapefruit popcorn? Every bite was sour and slimy, and the ghost peppers made me breathe fire."

"Eww! Gross!" I cried. Now my stomach was starting to feel sick. There's nothing worse than wet popcorn.

When we turned onto our block, I had a new idea. "What if your parents watched a cooking show? They could learn to make a lot of good food."

Desmond laughed. "Have you ever met my parents? They only like to make new and different things in the kitchen. And they never follow recipes."

"That's it!" I yelled. "Dr. Ackula said that you *have* to cook a family *recipe* for the project! We can look up a recipe online, and your parents have to follow it!"

Desmond's eyes lit up. "Andres, you're a genius!"

When we got home, Desmond told
his mom about Family Food Day.
Mrs. Cole jumped up and down.

"How exciting!" she exclaimed.
"Let's see what we have in the fridge.
I'm sure we can make the most
amazing family surprise dish ever!"

In a flash, Mrs. Cole dug into the refrigerator and pulled out old fish, vanilla frosting, hot mustard, broccoli, and liver. I couldn't imagine what those ingredients might make, and I didn't want to know!

"Um, Mrs. Cole," I said before she could pull anything else out of the refrigerator, "Dr. Ackula said we need to follow a recipe."

Desmond and I looked at each other and held our breath. Would it work? What I said wasn't exactly true, but I had to help Desmond. And save our class from eating whatever Mrs. Cole was planning to make.

A disappointed look spread on Mrs. Cole's face. "A recipe? Really?"

Desmond nodded slowly. "The rules are the rules, Mom."

Mrs. Cole sighed. "Well, that changes everything. I think I have a cookbook somewhere around here."

We watched as Mrs. Cole opened cabinet after cabinet until she finally found a cookbook that was so old it was covered in dust and cobwebs.

"Here you go, boys," she said, handing the haunted-looking book to us.

Desmond and I smiled. Now that we had a cookbook, nothing could possibly go wrong.

CHAPTER FIVE

KITCHEN IMPOSSIBLE

Desmond opened the old, creaky cover. The pages were yellow, and there were no photos like in most cookbooks. Instead there were drawings of each recipe. It was more like an ancient wizard's spell book than a cookbook.

"Here's one. Macaroni and cheese," Desmond announced. Then he whispered to me, "Even my mom can't ruin this."

I nodded. It would be a breeze!

While Mrs. Cole boiled the water, Desmond and I grated the cheese. Desmond was being extra careful because he didn't want anything to go wrong.

We made the pasta first and drained the water in the sink. Things were going well so far.

The Coles' kitchen seemed kind of
normal for the first time ever.

We put the noodles into a deep dish and added milk, cheese, and a cracked egg. Well, we probably should have let Mrs. Cole crack the egg because we got some of the shell in the macaroni. Okay, maybe *a lot* of the shell. But hopefully nobody would notice the extra *crunch*.

Mrs. Cole put the dish in the oven, and we set the timer. As the macaroni and cheese baked, Desmond and I did the rest of our homework. It was hard to concentrate, though, because Desmond's kitchen smelled DELICIOUS!

The wonderful aroma carried us over to the oven. We stared through the little window and watched the golden cheese ooze into bubbles and pop.

"Ooh, that looks yummy," I said.

"Yeah, right?" Desmond agreed. "I can't believe something this good is cooking in *my* house!"

When the timer went off, both of us were drooling. Desmond's mom pulled the mac and cheese out of the oven and placed it on the stove. She leaned over to smell it and shook her head sadly.

"Oh, I'm sorry, honey," she told Desmond. "It's just so . . . ordinary. Next time we'll make something special."

When she left the room, Desmond said, "I don't know what she's talking about."

"This macaroni and cheese looks even better than it smells!" I replied.

I grabbed two forks, and we had just a little bite. The warm cheesy noodles melted in my mouth.

"Wow," we both whispered with joy. Desmond took another taste. "I always thought my kitchen was cursed. But if I can make food this good on my first try, maybe I should do *all* the cooking around here."

I took another bite, and so did Desmond. Then we took another. And another until . . . *we finished the whole thing!*

"Oh no!" I exclaimed. "Desmond! We just ate your homework! There's nothing to bring to school tomorrow!"

Desmond licked his lips and said, "Don't worry, Andres. I'll just have to make another batch of my world-famous mac and cheese. But you better get home to work on *your* homework project too."

Oh yeah, I thought. *I have more cooking to do!*

CHAPTER SIX

THE THANK-YOU BITE

SViiiiFFFF

As soon as I stepped into my house, my ghost buddy Zax flew over and sniffed me.

One sniff. Two sniffs. Then, like, a hundred sniffs!

"What are you doing?" I asked.

"Andres . . . you smell!" Zax said.

I didn't know what to say to that. "Um, thanks?"

Zax took another whiff. "No, I mean, you smell yummy! Do I detect a hint of mac and cheese?"

"Oh yeah," I said. "I ate some over at Desmond's house."

That ghost just started laughing at me. "Impossible! Desmond's parents would never cook something that smells this good. Tell me the truth."

"That is the truth," I told him. "Desmond cooked the mac and cheese. As a matter of fact, he's making another batch right now."

In the blink of an eye, Zax flew through the wall and headed straight to Desmond's house.

He didn't even say good-bye.

My parents were in the kitchen. I was still so full from all that mac and cheese, I didn't want to have to think about cooking again, but I had no choice.

When I told my parents about my homework assignment, my dad got really excited.

"That's a fantastic project, son," he said. "What do you want to make?"

I didn't have to think about it for more than two seconds. "I want to make Mom's famous pork tacos with your secret salsa, Dad."

Dad clapped his hands together and said, "Then let's get chopping!"

I have to admit, Desmond was right. My parents *are* the opposite of his. Mine are really great chefs. And they aren't afraid to make a mess.

A *real* mess!

We chopped tomatoes, onion, peppers, and, of course, Dad's secret ingredient: garlic. Okay, okay, I know most salsa has garlic, but Dad uses so much garlic, your breath smells for weeks. It doesn't matter how many times you brush your teeth!

While the pork roasted, we made our own corn tortillas. And that just added to the mess.

When we were finally done, the kitchen looked like *we* were inside a taco. A very large, totally overstuffed taco!

"Let's take a break and relax for a little while," Mom said. "We can clean up later."

I was happy to hear that because cleaning this much mess would take forever.

Unless you have a ghost like Zax.

As soon as my parents left the room, he floated back in, and his eyes nearly popped out of his head.

But the weird thing was, Zax was thrilled by what he saw.

"Oh, Andres, you are full of surprises today," he cried. "First, you send me over to Desmond's house for the yummiest mac and cheese. And now you made the grossest, most fantastic mess for me to clean up in a completely wrecked kitchen! Talk about the BEST DAY EVER!"

Zax moved so fast, I had to jump out of his way. He spun around the kitchen like a tiny tornado sucking up all the mess like a vacuum. Dirty dishes, pans, and silverware were cleaned, and then they magically floated back in the cabinets and the drawers.

The whole place was spotless in a matter of seconds.

Before I could say thanks, Zax gave me a wink and disappeared through the ceiling.

When my parents came back in, their eyes almost popped out of their heads.

"Andres!" Mom said as she looked around the room and beamed with joy. "You've done a wonderful job cleaning the kitchen."

"And so fast," Dad added. "I think someone just earned himself a new chore."

Yep. That's how I got stuck with the job of cleaning the kitchen after every meal. Luckily, I have a secret ghost who loves doing all the dirty work.

CHAPTER SEVEN

RECIPE FOR DISASTER

Have you ever tried to ride your bike to school while balancing a bunch of tacos and salsa on a serving platter?

Well, it was a first time for me, I can tell you that!

Luckily, I'm a good bike rider. Desmond was riding a lot better too.

When we got to class, we had to put our food on one of the tables. Everyone's food smelled so good. I hoped we wouldn't have to wait too long to start eating!

Dr. Ackula looked more excited than I'd ever seen him.

"Okay, class," he said. "I'd like everyone to come to the front of the room and tell us what you brought for Family Food Day."

One by one, each kid talked about what they brought and why it was their favorite dish.

There were egg rolls, barbecue, shrimp salad, steamed dumplings, curried chickpeas, sweet potatoes stuffed with bacon, and even fried chicken and waffles.

And there were desserts, too. Glazed donuts, chocolate brownies, cookies, flan, and candy apples. Everything was so colorful.

Of course, Carla Bree brought a stinky cheese plate. But she ate stinky cheese every day, so there wasn't anything new about that.

As each kid spoke, I noticed that Dr. Ackula was drooling. At first, it was just a little. But then it was Jaylen Torche's turn to present.

"I brought steak," he said. "And my mom always says when you cook steak, it has to be medium rare. That way it's nice and juicy."

Now Dr. Ackula's mouth was slobbering, and he nearly fell out of his chair. Finally he grabbed a napkin and wiped away the drool.

"I have heard enough, children," Dr. Ackula said quickly. "No more presentations. It's time to feast!"

I hadn't even gotten to talk about my dish, but that didn't matter. I was ready to dig in!

And so was everyone else. We ate
and ate and ate until I thought we
were going to burst.

I thought Desmond Cole would
have the biggest plate for sure, but I
was wrong.

Dr. Ackula ate *way* more than Desmond. He got to every dish first and sank those sharp teeth of his into everyone's special meal.

Our teacher was eating so much, the whole class actually stopped just to watch him in action. It looked like he was in an eating competition . . . with himself!

When he noticed my tacos, Dr. Ackula chomped down on four of them at the same time. Then he let out a little burp, and a real serious look spread across his face.

"Who made these?" he demanded.

I raised my hand slowly.

"What are they, Andres?" he asked, burping again.

"It's my mom's famous pork tacos with my dad's secret salsa," I said, smiling proudly.

Before I could answer, he ate four more tacos. "These are amazing! I've never tasted anything like this before! There's a taste I can't place in the salsa. What is it?"

"That's the secret ingredient," I said. "It's lots and lots of garlic."

As soon as I said the word "garlic," Dr. Ackula froze mid-bite. His eyes started to water, and there was a gurgling sound coming from his stomach. And then it happened.

Dr. Ackula farted!

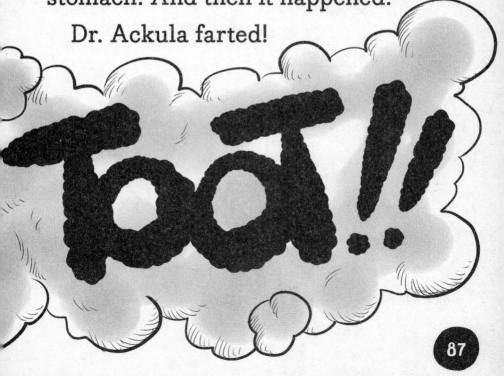

CHAPTER EIGHT

CLASSROOM PEST

It's a good thing people can't smell stories, because Dr. Ackula's fart smelled so, *so* foul.

How foul? you ask.

It was so foul that Carla's stinky cheese melted into smelly gooey globs.

It was so foul that Jaylen passed out.

It was so foul that the classroom windows fogged up with a greenish yellow color.

And then Dr. Ackula farted again!

"I'm sorry, class," he apologized. "I've never eaten garlic before. Does it normally make you, um, *toot* like this?"

Everyone held their nose and shook their head. Because *no way* had garlic ever made us stink up a place like that. Right then, Dr. Ackula let out another, well, let's just call it a *toot* to be nice. And, no lie, a little cloud of smoke came out of the back of his pants.

We watched as the stink smog floated over the class. We dived to the ground to avoid it, but that cloud had a mind of its own. It was out to get us, so we scattered.

Desmond and I hid behind the bookcase.

"I have an idea," he whispered.

Then Desmond jumped up and grabbed two crusty loaves of bread from the food table. He opened the window and fanned the bread in the air, trying to get the cloud outside.

But it didn't work.

Nope. That cloud landed right on our class pet's cage. Some of the kids screamed as the cage rattled and the cover started to come off. I might have screamed too, but I was too busy backing up as far away as I could get.

I didn't know what was under that cover, but I didn't want to be anywhere near it when we found out.

Suddenly a huge pair of black wings burst out of the cage. A shadow beast took flight around the room, screeching wildly.

Our class pet was a bat!

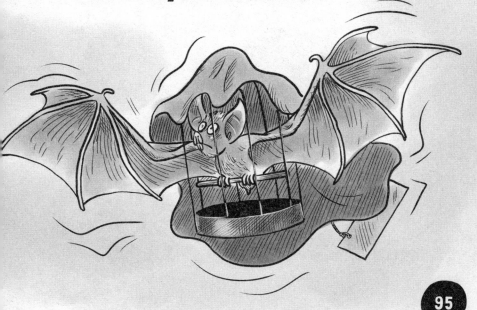

Now it was my turn to scream, and I turned to run. Only I didn't get far because I crashed right into the food table. Family Food Day spilled all over me! Including Carla's stinky, melted cheese. Yuck!

Desmond was holding the door so everybody in our class could escape.

Soon we were the last ones in the classroom along with a wild bat, a stink cloud, and Dr. Ackula.

"Stop!" Dr. Ackula called out as he pulled down the candlestick on his desk like a lever!

Stone walls dropped down out of nowhere and blocked all of the exits! The doors were gone. The windows were gone. And all the sunlight was gone.

The room was dark except for a few candles flickering from a holder that was in the corner.

Desmond and I looked at each other.

"What is going on here?" I whispered, and I could feel my legs getting kind of shaky.

"Andres," Desmond said, "all I know is that we're trapped."

CHAPTER NINE

SECONDS

With the crusty bread still in his hands, Desmond turned his attention to the bat flapping and screeching above our heads.

He waved the bread around, trying to defend us from the beast.

But that bat didn't care.

I have been in A LOT of weird situations. But there we were, trapped in our classroom that had somehow turned into a stone castle, with our teacher who was looking more and more like a vampire.

I mean, could things *get* weirder?
While Desmond kept the bat away,
Dr. Ackula cried, "Wait! Put down
your bread. I love Seconds!"

Desmond froze.

"Seconds?" he asked. "How could you possibly want seconds now? Haven't you eaten enough food already?"

"Yeah," I agreed. "You ate half of what everybody brought for Family Food Day. There was barely anything left for the class!"

"I'm not talking about food," Dr. Ackula said. "Seconds is the name of my bat. He's my best friend, and I love him. Waving around that bread is freaking him out."

Freaking him *out?* I thought. We were the ones getting freaked out by an out-of-control bat!

Who even has *a pet bat?*

Desmond put down the bread, and Seconds fluttered over to Dr. Ackula's shoulder.

"Kids," our teacher said, "I owe you an explanation."

But I was pretty sure I had this mystery figured out.

"It's cool, Dr. Ackula," I said. "We get it. You're a vampire, right?"

"A *what*?!" Dr. Ackula chuckled. "Don't be silly, Andres. What would make you think that?"

"Are you serious?" I yelled. "Look at all the clues! You have secret

stone walls that block sunlight from the room. You have a bat for a best friend. And you are way allergic to garlic!"

"Plus, your name is DR. ACKULA! Like Dracula!" Desmond added.

"Hmmm," Dr. Ackula said with a pause. "I can see why you boys are confused. But there's a perfectly good reason for everything."

That's when Dr. Ackula answered all of our questions.

He told us that the stone walls were for Seconds. The bat slept all day, but he liked to fly around the classroom at night. Dr. Ackula was afraid he would fly away, so he had the stone walls built to block the windows and door.

"I just wanted to keep him safe," Dr. Ackula said.

"I guess that makes sense," Desmond said.

"But what about the garlic?" I asked.

"Oh that," Dr. Ackula said, embarrassed. "I don't think I'm the only person in the world who can't eat garlic. It's quite delicious, but it gives me tummy troubles."

Desmond laughed. "I'll say!"

"What about your name?" I asked Dr. Ackula.

"That's just an odd stroke of luck," he responded. "I mean, before I went to medical school and became a doctor, I was just Mr. Ackula."

Desmond's shoulders slumped, and he actually looked a little bummed that our teacher *wasn't* a vampire.

"So, does this mean you're just a normal teacher?" Desmond asked.

"I'm afraid so," Dr. Ackula said. "I'm just your average teacher with a pet bat, a secret castle, and a bad case of the farts."

With that, all three of us burst out laughing. Even Seconds seemed to get in on the fun!

CHAPTER TEN

JUST DESSERTS

Now that Desmond can cook, he likes to make treats for Seconds and Dr. Ackula. And let me tell you, that teacher can *eat!*

Desmond's parents help him cook sometimes. Of course, they think the recipes need more *flair!*

Last week they added olives and black licorice to the turkey chili recipe.

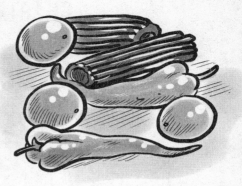

And yesterday Desmond's mother thought the chocolate-chip-cookie recipe wasn't exciting enough. So she added liver and sauerkraut to it. Good thing Seconds eats everything!

The funny thing is, Dr. Ackula eats everything too!

Well, everything except garlic.
Nobody wants him to eat *that* again!

And you know what's great about having a teacher who likes your food? He's always happy to help you with your homework during lunch and after school.

It turns out, having a maybe-vampire eat my homework may have been the best thing to ever happen to my report card!